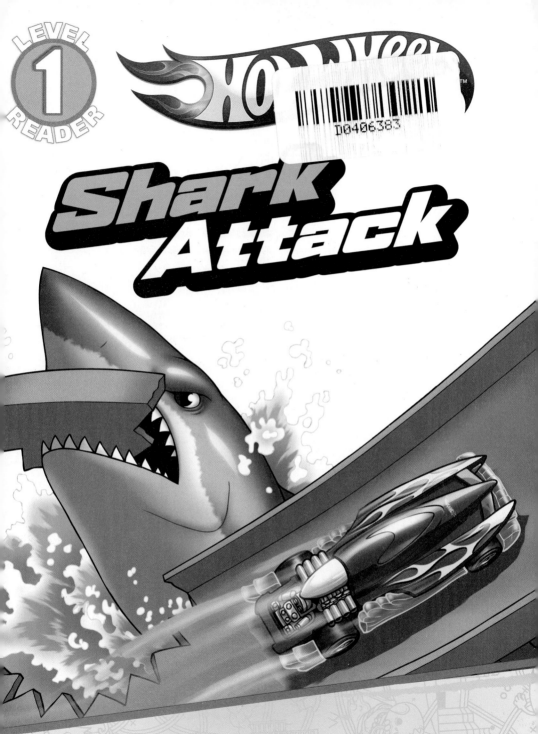

Shark Attack

By Ace Landers
Illustrated by Dave White

SCHOLASTIC INC.

ISBN 978-0-545-46824-4

HOT WHEELS and associated trademarks and trade dress are owned by, and used under
license from Mattel. Inc. © 2013 Mattel, Inc. All Rights Reserved.

Published by Scholastic Inc. SCHOLASTIC and associated logos
are trademarks and/or registered trademarks of Scholastic Inc.

12 11 10 9 8 7 6 5 4   14 15 16 17/0

Printed in the U.S.A.   40
First printing, September 2013

What track is Team Hot Wheels trying today?

The Triple Track Twister racetrack!

Drivers must rocket through three loops over the ocean.

BEWARE OF SHARKS

The blue driver sees a sign.
This is a dangerous track.

BEWARE
OF
SHARKS

The red driver is ready for a thrill ride.

Team Red races down the pier.

The blue driver tries to warn him. But it is too late!

The first loop is fast.

The second loop is faster.

The third loop is a
surprise. Shark attack!

A shark jumps up and
snaps at the red driver.

The red driver swerves.

A second shark leaps out of the water! Look out!

Team Red escapes
the shark.

The track is not so lucky.

The red driver warns the yellow driver.

But the yellow driver wants a turn. He has a surprise for the sharks.

The yellow driver jolts
around the first loop.
There are no sharks.

There are no sharks on the second loop.

Here comes the third loop.
Where are the sharks?

Both sharks jump up and attack!

They have sharp teeth!

But the yellow driver has a car with a bite of its own!

Both sharks are really scared!

They swim away.

But now the yellow driver is going too fast!

He skids over the broken track, spins around . . .

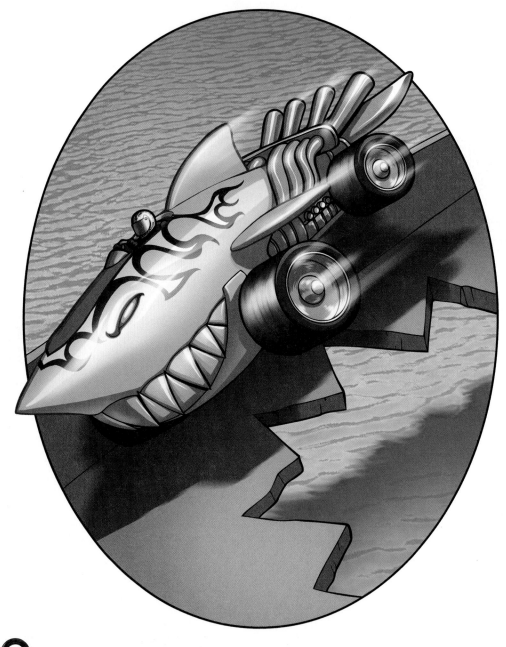

. . . and crosses the finish line backward!

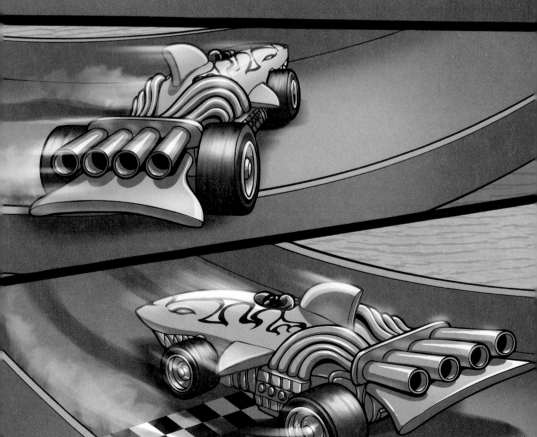

Thanks to Team Hot Wheels, the track is safe from shark attacks!